FREAKY
FAMILIES

Diana Wynne Jones

FREAKY FAMILIES

Illustrated by Marion Lindsay

HarperCollins *Children's Books*

First published in paperback in Great Britain by
HarperCollins *Children's Books* in 2014
HarperCollins *Children's Books* is a division of HarperCollins*Publishers*
Ltd, 77-85 Fulham Palace Road, Hammersmith, London, W6 8JB.

The HarperCollins *Children's Books* website address is:
www.harpercollins.co.uk

www.dianawynnejones.com

1

ISBN 978-0-00-750762-7

Printed and bound in England by Clays Ltd, St Ives plc.

Contents

Granny One

Granny Two

Granny Three

Granny Four

Erg and Emily

Teddy

Aunt Bea

Simon, Debbie and Nancy

Honey

The Four
Grannies

Chapter One

Erg's Dad and Emily's Mum found
they had to go away to a Conference
for four days, leaving Erg and Emily at
home.

"I want a house to come back to,"
said Erg's Dad, thinking of the time Erg

had borrowed the front door to make an underground fort in the garden.

"We'd better ask one of the Grannies to come and look after them," said Emily's Mum, knowing that if Erg did not borrow a thing, Emily could be trusted to fall over it and break it. Emily was younger than Erg, but she was enormous. She needed bigger shoes than Erg's Dad.

There were four Grannies to choose from, because Erg's Dad and Emily's Mum had both been divorced before they married one another.

Granny One was strict. She wore her hair scraped back from her forbidding face and her favourite saying was, "Life is always saying No." 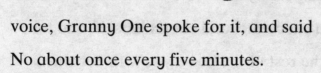 Since Life did not have a voice, Granny One spoke for it, and said No about once every five minutes.

Granny Two was a worrier. She could worry about anything. She was fond of ringing up in the middle of the night to ask if Emily was getting enough

vitamins, or – in her special, hushed worrying voice – if Erg ought to be sent to a Special School.

Granny Three was very rich and very stingy. She was the one Emily hated most. Granny Three always arrived with a big box of chocolates. She would give Erg's Dad a chocolate, and Emily's Mum a chocolate, and eat six herself, and take the rest of the box away with her when she went. Erg agreed with Emily that this was mean, but he thought Granny Three was more fun than the others, because she had a new car and different coloured

hair every time she came.

Granny Four was a saint. She was gentle and quavery and wrinkled. If Erg and Emily quarrelled in front of her, or even spoke loudly, Granny Four promptly came over faint and had to have a doctor.

Granny Four was the one Erg and Emily chose to look after them. If you could avoid making Granny Four feel faint she usually let you do what you wanted. But, when Emily's Mum rang Granny Four to ask her, Granny Four was faint already. She had been let down

over a Save The Children Bazaar and
was too ill to come.

So, despite the shrill groans of Erg
and the huge moans of Emily, Emily's
Mum phoned Granny One. To Erg's
relief, Granny One was going on holiday
and could not come either. So that left
Granny Two, because Granny Three had
never been known to look after anyone
but herself. But Erg's Dad phoned
Granny Three, all the same, hoping she
might pay for someone to look after
Erg and Emily. Granny Three said she
thought it was an excellent idea for

Emily and Erg to look after themselves.

Erg's Dad phoned Granny Two.

"What!" exclaimed Granny Two, hushed and worried. "Leave dear Erg and poor little Emily all alone, for all that time!"

"But we're only going to Scotland for four days," Erg's Dad protested.

"I know, dear," said Granny Two. "But I'm thinking of *you*. Scotland is covered with oil these days and *so* dangerous!"

Erg and Emily were not looking forward to Granny Two. They waved their parents off gloomily, and sat about

waiting for Granny Two to arrive. She was a long time coming. Emily fidgeted round the living room like an impatient horse, knocking things over right and left. Erg felt an idea coming on. He wandered away to the kitchen to see what he could find.

All the food was wrapped up and carefully labelled so that Granny Two could find it, but Erg found a biscuit-tin. It had holes in the lid from the time he had started a caterpillar farm. Inside were the works of a clock he had once borrowed. It seemed a good beginning

for an invention. He collected other
things: an egg-beater, the blades off
the mixer, a sardine-tin-opener, and a
skewer. He took them all back to the
living-room and began fitting them
together. The invention was already
looking quite promising, when the phone
rang. Emily bounced up to answer it,
and, quite naturally, she trod on the
invention as she went and squashed it
flat. Erg roared with rage.

It was Granny Two on the phone.
"I'm terribly sorry, dear. I'd got halfway,
when I thought I'd left my kitchen tap

on. I'm just setting out again now."

"*Was* your tap on?" asked Emily.

"No, dear. But just suppose it had been."

Emily went back to the living room to find Erg still roaring with rage. "Look what you've done! You've ruined my invention!"

Emily looked at the invention. It looked like a squashed biscuit-tin with egg-beaters sticking out of it. "It's only a squashed biscuit-tin," she said. "And you ought to put those egg-beaters back."

But Erg had just discovered that the

hand-beater fitted beautifully into a split in the side of the biscuit-tin.

"You're not supposed to have any of them," said Emily. But Erg took no notice. He wound the handle of the egg-beater. The battered metal of the tin went in and out as if it were breathing, and the pieces of clock inside made a most interesting noise. Emily got annoyed at the way Erg had forgotten her. "Put those things *back, you horrible little boy*!" she roared.

She was trampling towards Erg to take the invention apart, when a shocked

voice said, "Emily! *Children!*"

They looked round to find Granny Four in the doorway. She was pale and quavery and threatening to faint.

Chapter Two

Erg and Emily tried to stop Granny Four fainting by smiling politely. "I thought you weren't coming," said Erg.

"I couldn't leave you two poor children all alone," Granny Four said in a failing voice.

Emily and Erg looked at one another.
Neither of them had quite the courage
to say Granny Two was already on her
way.

"Here you are, dear," Granny Four
said to Emily. Shakily, she held out a
small, elderly book. "This will put you in
a better frame of mind. It's a beautiful
little book about a wicked little girl
called Emily. You'll find it charming,
dear."

Emily took the book. It was not the
kind of gift you could say thank you
for easily. "I'll take it upstairs to read,"

Emily said, and thundered away so as
not to seem ungrateful.

Erg was hoping heartily that Granny
Four had something better for him. But
it was not much better. It was a shiny red
stick, narrower at one end than the other.

"I think it's a chopstick," said Granny
Four. "It was in the Bazaar." She must
have seen from Erg's expression that he
was not loving the chopstick particularly.
She went white and leant against the
side of the door. "You can pretend
it's a magic wand, dear," she said
reproachfully

Erg knew she would faint. He took the chopstick hurriedly and jammed it in one of the holes in his invention. It must have caught in the works of the clock inside the squashed tin, because, when he wound the handle of the egg-beater, the skewer, the sardine-tin-opener and the mixer-blades all began to turn round, grating and clanking as they turned. It was much more interesting now.

27

Granny Four smothered a slight yawn and began to look healthier. "We can take such delight in simple things!" she said.

But, just then, a voice shouted "Coo-ee!" and Granny Two staggered in. She had brought four bags of potatoes, two dozen oranges and a packet of health-food. Granny Four took in the situation and turned faint again. Granny Two took in Granny Four and sprang to her side. "You shouldn't have come, dear. You look ready to collapse! Come upstairs and lie down and I'll make you

a nice cup of tea." And she led Granny Four away.

Erg was rather pleased. It looked as if the two Grannies could keep one another busy while he got on with his invention. He went into the kitchen again. This time he collected the cutters from the mincer, the handle of the hot tap, the knobs off the cooker, and the clip that held the bag of the vacuum cleaner together. Most of these things stuck into the holes on top of the biscuit-tin. When Erg wound the egg-beater this time, the tap top, the mincer-cutters and the cooker knobs all twiddled

round and round, quite beautifully.
The works of the clock clanked. The tin
breathed in and out. And everything
ground and grated just like a real
machine.

Erg was trying to find a place for the
clip from the vacuum cleaner, when
he looked up into the outraged face of
Granny One.

Granny One! Erg looked up again
unbelievingly. She was really there. She
was putting down her neat suitcase in
order to fold her arms grimly.

"You're on holiday!" he said.

"I cancelled my holiday," Granny One said grimly. "To look after you. Take all those things back to the kitchen at once."

"But you're on holiday," Erg argued. "You can have a holiday from saying No, if you like."

"Life is always saying No," said Granny One. "Take those things back."

"If Life is always saying No," Erg argued reasonably, "it's saying No to me taking them back too."

But Granny One tapped the floor with her knobby shoe, quite impervious to reason. "I'm waiting. Do as you're told."

"Oh, bother you!" said Erg.

That was a mistake. It brought a storm down on Erg's head. It started with "Don't you speak to me like that!" and ended with Erg sullenly carrying the invention out into the hall to take it to pieces in the kitchen.

The noise fetched Granny Two down the stairs. She stared at Granny One. "What are *you* doing here?" said Granny Two.

"My duty," said Granny One. "I've come to look after the children."

"So have I," said Granny Two. "I can

manage perfectly."

"Of course you can't," said Granny One. "You fuss all the time, and you spoil the children."

"And you," said Granny Two, "are cruel to them."

Granny One had her mouth open to make a blistering reply, when Granny Four tottered down the stairs, faintly wringing her hands. Granny One pointed at her unbelievingly. "Is *she* here too?"

"Yes, dear, but she can't manage on her own," said Granny Two.

"Indeed I can!" Granny Four

quavered, clinging to the stair-rail.

"It's just as well I came," Granny One said grimly. "I see I shall have to look after the lot of you."

"I do not need looking after!" Grannies Two and Four said in chorus.

By this time it was clear to Erg that three Grannies kept one another even busier than two. Much relieved, he went into the kitchen. There he put the hot tap top back, and the knobs from the cooker, because he knew Granny One would notice those. Then he went out of the back door and into the living room by the French window and hid the invention safely behind the sofa. Then he went out into the hall again. The Grannies were still insulting one another.

"I didn't know you all hated one another," he said.

To his surprise, this stopped the argument at once. All the Grannies turned and assured Erg that they loved one another very much. Then they turned and assured one another. After which, they all went into the kitchen for a cup of tea.

Erg went back to work on his

invention behind the sofa. The clip off
the vacuum cleaner fitted nicely on the
end of the sardine-tin-opener. But the
invention needed something else to
make it perfect. Erg could not think what
it needed. He could not think clearly,
because the Grannies were now going
up and down stairs, calling out about
potatoes and rattling at doors.

Finally, Granny Two came into the
living room. "Erg, dear – Oh dear! He's
vanished too. I'm so worried."

"No I haven't," Erg said, bobbing up
from behind the sofa. "I'm playing at

hiding," he explained, before Granny Two could ask, "What's the matter?"

"Emily's locked herself in the bathroom, dear. Be a dear and go and get her out."

Chapter Three

Erg sighed and went upstairs. But it was not a wasted journey. The thought of the bathroom put into his head exactly what would make the invention perfect. It needed glass tubes, with blue water bubbling in them, going *plotterta-plotterta*

like inventions did in films. He banged at the bathroom door.

"Go away!" boomed Emily from inside. She sounded tearful. "I'm busy. I'm reading Granny Four's book."

"Why are you doing it in there?" Erg asked.

"Because they keep interrupting and asking where to put potatoes and oranges."

"They want you to come out."

"I'm not going to," Emily

boomed. "Not till I've read it. It's beautiful. It's ever so sad." Erg could hear her sobbing as he went away downstairs.

He went to the kitchen, where the Grannies were sitting among mounds of potatoes and oranges, and told them Emily was reading.

He thought he would never understand Grannies. One by one, they tiptoed to the bathroom, rattled the handle and whispered there was a cup of tea outside. "And don't hurt your eyes, dear," Granny Two whispered. "I'm pushing a

biscuit under the door for you."

It seemed to be keeping them busy.
Erg sat behind the sofa and got on with
thinking how to make blue water go
plotterta-plotterta. But he had still not
worked it out when Granny Four came
and quavered to him that Emily had

not touched her tea. Nor had he when
Granny Two came to tell him that Emily
was ruining her eyes. Nor had he when
Granny One came and told him to go out
and get some nice fresh air.

Erg was annoyed. He wished he
had thought of locking himself in the

bathroom too. And he was even more
annoyed when Emily at last came
out. She came straight to the sofa and
crashed heavily down on it with her chin
resting on the back.

"What are you making, dear brother?"
she said in a sweet cooing voice.

Erg looked up at her suspiciously.
There were tear-streaks down Emily's
face and an expression on it even more
saintly than Granny Four's. "What's the
matter with you?" he said.

Emily turned her eyes piously to the
ceiling. "I have taken a vow to be good,

dear brother," she said. "It was that
beautiful sad book Granny Four gave
me. The girl in it was called Emily too,
and she was terribly punished for her
wickedness."

"Go away," said Erg. He was not sure
he could bear it if Emily was going to be
a saint as well as Granny Four.

"Ah, dear brother," cooed Emily,
"do not spurn me. I must stay and pray
for you. You have wickedly taken all
the kitchen things for that Thing you're
making."

"It's not a Thing!" Erg said angrily.

Up till now he had not truly considered
what his invention was, but Emily so
annoyed him that he said rudely, "It's a
prayer-machine. You wind the handle
and it answers your prayer."

"Sinful boy!" Emily said, with her eyes
on the ceiling again. "Let us pray. I pray
that my beloved brother Erchenwald
Randolph Gervase turns into a good
boy—"

That was the most dreadful insult. Erg
lost his temper. Usually when people said
his string of terrible names, he hit them,
but Emily was so much bigger than he

was that he had never yet dared hit her.
Instead, in a frenzy, he wound at the
egg-beater. The squashed tin breathed in
and out. The works of the clock ground
and crunched inside. The chopstick
revolved. The skewer twiddled. The
sardine-opener and the mincer-cutters
wobbled and whirled. Erg wound
furiously: *pray pray pray praypraypray.*
"Take Emily away!" he shouted. "I don't
want her!"

In the midst of the noise, he thought he
heard Emily stop being a saint and start
shouting at him like she usually did. But

he did not stop winding. *Pray pray pray praypraypray.*

When at last his arm became too tired to go on, he left off winding and looked up to glare at Emily. She was not there. In her place, with its chin resting on the back of the sofa, was a large yellow teddy bear.

Chapter Four

Erg stared at the teddy. The bear stared back at him. There was a sorrowful expression in its glass eyes and reproach written all over its yellow furry muzzle.

"Go away," Erg said to it. "You're not

Emily. You're just pretending."

But the bear remained, leaning on the back of the sofa, staring reproachfully.

Erg took an alarmed look at his invention. *Could* it be a prayer-machine? Could the chopstick perhaps really be a magic wand? These things just did not happen. On the other hand, he had never seen the teddy before in his life, and its furry face did look remarkably like Emily's. It was big too, about as much too large for a teddy as Emily was for a girl. Erg tried not to think of what the Grannies would say. He got up

and searched the living room. Then he searched the garden. Emily was nowhere in either. Erg went out into the hall to search the rest of the house.

He stopped short. The front door was wide open. Granny Three was coming in through it lugging bright red suitcases. Granny Three, of all people! Erg stared. Granny Three's hair was a pale baby pink this time, and the new car outside in the road was bright snake green.

"There's no need to stare," Granny Three said to him. "I've come to look after you. Have you seen Emily?"

"No," said Erg, trying hard not to look guilty.

"Why not?" said Granny Three. "I've brought her such a sweet dress." She put the suitcases down and picked up a dress from the hall stand. Erg blinked. It was a very small dress. It did not look as if it would fit the teddy bear, let alone Emily.

Still, this was the first time Granny Three had ever been known to give anyone anything.

The kitchen door opened and Grannies Four, Two and One looked out to see what was happening.

Granny Three took Granny Four in
and, behind her, the unwelcoming faces
of Grannies Two and One. She patted
her pink hair and drew herself up tall. "I
had to come," she said. "My conscience
wouldn't let me leave those two poor
children alone."

Erg was interested to hear that
Granny Three thought she had a
conscience. He always thought he
inherited his lack of conscience from
Granny Three. He looked at the other
Grannies to see what they thought.

Grannies Two and One did indeed

draw breath as if they intended to say something thoroughly crushing, but then they looked at Erg and did not say it. Grannies Three and Four looked at Erg too. All four put on sweet smiles.

And Erg felt horrible. He discovered he must have a conscience too. He could not think why else he should feel so guilty about that teddy bear. Granny Three said brightly, "Well, what can I do? I brought my apron." Erg crept away from them upstairs and searched the rest of the house. But Emily was not anywhere. And when Erg went

downstairs again, the teddy still sat
accusingly on the sofa. Erg was forced to
believe that he had indeed turned Emily
into a teddy bear.

He dared not tell the Grannies.
When they called him to lunch, he said,
"Emily's locked in the bathroom again."

"But she'll miss her dinner," quavered
Granny Four.

Granny Three, who had settled in as if
she had always lived there, said, "Then
there'll be more for us. No, dear," she
added to Granny One, "you must always
mash potatoes with cream. I brought

some cream."

Granny Two could not take the matter so calmly. "We must get Emily out before she grows up peculiar!" she said, and she set off upstairs to the bathroom.

Erg raced up with her and was just in time to wedge the landing carpet under the door so that it would not open. He left Granny Two there rattling and calling and raced down to the living room. The teddy still sat there, vast and yellow, on the sofa. But Erg felt it would be just like Emily to turn into something else while he was not looking. Then he

might not be able to find her to turn
her back. He decided to take the teddy
in to lunch with him. That was terrible.
Granny Three actually smiled kindly.
Granny Four took the teddy and sat
it in a chair of its own. "Is it a teddy-
weddy then?" she said, and pretended
to feed the teddy with mashed potato.
Granny One kept looking from Erg to
the teddy to Granny Four and snorting
sarcastically. And when Granny Two
came downstairs, she said, "Oh, the
fairies have brought you a teddy! How
exciting!"

In between all this, all the Grannies wondered where Emily was and said she was growing up peculiar.

But halfway through lunch, Erg noticed the glass salt-cellar, and he saw the way out of his troubles. Let him put that salt-cellar upside down, with a drinking-straw in it. Let both be filled with blue water going *plotterta-plotterta*. And Erg knew the machine would answer his prayer and turn the teddy back into Emily again. The trouble was, could he do it before the Grannies noticed that the teddy's reproachful face

was exactly like Emily's?

Erg knew that he was going to have to
keep all four Grannies very busy.

Chapter Five

When lunch was over, the Grannies all put on aprons to wash up. Erg said he would take some lunch to Emily. Granny One sternly handed him two oranges.

"Eat those for vitamins," she said.

"That's right, dear," agreed Granny

Two. "Push Emily's under the door for
her."

Erg went upstairs and parked the
teddy and the lunch in the bath. Then
he wedged the door again and went
down to the living room. He peeled
both oranges and broke the peel into
very small bits, which he scattered all
over the carpet. But it takes a lot to
keep four Grannies busy. Erg was still
gulping and feeling much too full of
orange, when Granny One escaped
from the washing up and stood in the
doorway staring grimly at the bits of

orange peel.

"I'll use the vacuum cleaner on it, shall I?" Erg said brightly.

"No you will not," said Granny One. She went and got the vacuum cleaner herself and firmly plugged it in.

Erg watched expectantly as she switched it on. Since the clip that held the bag together was now part of the prayer-machine, there was nothing to hold the dust in the cleaner at all. Dust came out in a cloud, like an explosion. Big wads of dirt followed it. And after that came orange peel,

whirling and whizzing. Granny One switched the cleaner off in a hurry and screamed for help.

Granny Four hurried in and turned faint in the dust. Granny Three came and turned the vacuum cleaner upside down. All the rest of the dust fell out of it.

"I don't understand these things," Granny Three said fretfully. "Telephone for a man."

"Pull out the plug first!" gasped Granny Two, hastening to the scene. "There's electricity leaking into it all the time!"

"Nonsense!" snapped Granny One, coming to her senses. "Erg, what have you done to this machine?"

But Erg was already tip-toeing into the kitchen. Hastily, he unscrewed the salt-cellar and poured the salt into the nearest thing – which happened to be the sugar bowl. He snatched up a packet of transparent drinking-straws. Finally, he turned the tap on over the half-finished washing up. It was not long before bubbly water was pouring over on to the floor. Erg turned the tap off again.

"Hey!" he yelled. "You left the tap running!"

This fetched all four Grannies back at a gallop.

Satisfied, Erg went back into the dust-hung living room and collected the invention from behind the sofa. He took it up to the bathroom and locked himself in with it and the salt-cellar and the straws and the teddy and Emily's lunch. He thought he had given himself an hour's peace at least.

But it takes more than dust and water to keep four Grannies busy. Ten minutes

later, Granny Four was rattling at the bathroom door. "Emily, dear, are you all right?"

"It's me in here now," Erg called. "Emily's gone for a walk."

"Then could you let me in, dear?" Granny Four called back. "I'd like a little wash before I go for my rest."

"You can't *rest*!" Erg called. He was horrified. Next thing he knew, they would all be up here, fussing about with cups of tea and hot-water-bottles and things.

"Why not, dear?" quavered Granny Four.

Erg cast about for a reason. His eye fell on the washing-basket. "There's all the washing to do," he shouted. "I'll bring it downstairs for you, shall I?"

"I'd better go and tell them," quavered Granny Four and tottered away.

But, when Erg looked in the washing-basket, it was empty. Nothing daunted, Erg took off the clothes he was wearing and put them in the basket. Grannies always said clothes were dirty when you had hardly worn them anyway. Then he went to Emily's room and his own and collected all the clothes he could find there. Erg unfolded them and scrunched them up in his hands and rammed them into the basket. Then he put on clean clothes and staggered downstairs with the basket.

"Here you are," he said, emptying the crumpled heap on the kitchen floor.

The four Grannies were gathered there eating chocolates out of the box Granny Three had brought. They gave the heap various looks of suffering and dismay. Granny Four turned pale. Granny Two sprang up saying she would fill the sink with nice hot water.

"You're allowed to use the washing-machine," Erg said.

"Oh no, dear," said Granny Two. "Electricity doesn't mix with water. It gets into the clothes, you know."

On reflection, Erg thought that washing in the sink would keep them busier. He took the basket back to the bathroom. Then he undid the toilet cistern and took out the blue block in it to make the blue water that was to go *plotterta-plotterta*. Then he thought he had better check to see how busy the Grannies were.

He peeped round the kitchen door
to find them quite out of control again.
Granny Three was standing in the heap
of clothes sorting them out. She took up
a shirt, shook it fiercely, and passed it
to Granny One. "This is clean too," she
said. "I think someone has been making
work for us."

"Quite right," said Granny One,
holding the shirt up to the light. "Clean
and ironed." She passed the shirt to
Granny Two, who smoothed it out
and folded it carefully and passed it to
Granny Four. Granny Four turned to put

the shirt on a large heap of others and saw Erg watching.

"Will you take these back upstairs, dear," she said.

"All right," said Erg. "And then I'll bring down the rest of the washing, shall I?"

"*Is* there more?" Granny Three asked, transferring her angry look from the next shirt to Erg.

"Oh yes," said Erg. There was going to be, if it killed him.

He went upstairs with the pile of clothes and locked himself in the

73

bathroom again. At least, Erg thought, he had kept the Grannies too busy to think of Emily for some time. But, at the rate they were going, they would be asking about her any minute now.

Erg took the plate of lunch out of the bath and used it to dirty ten of the shirts in the pile. But, though he spread

the lunch very thinly and carefully with his toothbrush, it would not go round more than ten shirts. He found himself looking longingly at his invention where it sat in the wash-basin. Even without the blue water, it had already worked quite well. Erg decided to give it another try.

He wound the egg-beater – *pray pray pray praypraypray*. The tin crunched in and out. The mixer-blades, the skewer and the sardine-opener grated and revolved. The vacuum cleaner clip, the mincer-cutters and the chopstick wobbled and twirled. "Make the washing keep them busy," Erg said, winding away.

Chapter Six

Erg's clean clothes had become quite well covered with lunch and the blue from the toilet-block. He took them off and put them in the basket with the ten shirts. In their place, he put on the first clothes left in the heap: Emily's

nightdress, his own jeans and Emily's school shirt. Dressed in this flowing raiment, he went down to the living room to roll in the dust there. But Granny Four was there, feebly flicking with a duster.

"What are you doing, dear?"

"Playing oil-sheiks," said Erg. He went out into the garden and rolled in a flower-bed.

Granny Four was not in the living room when he came back. To Erg's horror, she met him outside the bathroom, carrying the teddy. "You forgot teddy-weddy, dear."

It was awful how the Grannies kept getting out of control. Erg locked the door and took off the raiment. He put on the next things: Emily's tartan skirt and a frilly blouse. This time, he took the teddy with him and wedged the bathroom door shut.

"What are you doing now, dear?" asked Granny Four.

"Playing North Sea oil," Erg explained. "The teddy is my sporran." He went and rolled in the flower-bed again.

This time, he got safely back to the

bathroom. But he did not dare leave the teddy behind when he set out again in the next set of clothes, which were his own striped pyjamas.

"I'm playing going to bed," he told Granny Four before she could ask, and went and rolled in the flower-bed once more.

While he was rolling, Granny Two and Granny Three came into the garden with a basket of washing to hang on the clothes-line. They were struggling to hold a ballooning skirt and a kicking pair of jeans in what seemed a very strong

wind. Erg lay in the earth and watched. The skirt made a strong dive and almost got away. Both Grannies caught it. It took them some time to get it pegged, and the dress they took up next seemed to be blowing even harder. Erg licked one finger and thoughtfully held it up. There was almost no wind. Yet the row of things on the line were flapping and struggling and kicking as if there was half a gale.

Interesting. But where was Granny One? Erg got up and went through the back door into the kitchen to check on

Granny One. She was not there. But while Erg was looking round to make sure, the pile of wet washing on the draining board rolled heavily over and went *flap*, down on to the kitchen floor. Erg could see it oozing and trickling and spreading over the floor. He watched with interest. The washing was definitely working its way over towards the nearest heap of potatoes to get itself nice and dirty again.

Erg was delighted. This prayer-machine worked! He went upstairs in his earthy pyjamas, convinced that the chopstick

really must be some kind of magic wand.
He only needed to get the blue water
working, and he could turn Emily back
again.

But Granny One was outside the
bathroom door, knocking and rattling at
it. She turned and looked at Erg. He had
rarely seen her look so grim.

"Take those pyjamas off at *once*! What
are you and Emily—?"

"The washing," Erg said hastily, "has
fallen on the kitchen floor."

To his relief, Granny One pushed
past him and went rushing downstairs to

rescue the washing. Erg locked himself
in the bathroom again and put the teddy
back in the bath. He was beginning
to feel that four Grannies were too
much for any boy to control. There was
another annoying thing too. There were
no more of his own clothes left to wear.
He had got them all dirty. He stayed in
his pyjamas and got down to work on the
salt-cellar at last.

He had the salt-cellar nicely filled with
blue water, when he was interrupted
again, by quivering shouts from the
garden. Erg could not resist opening

the bathroom window to look. There
was washing all over the garden. Some
of it was blowing and kicking in the
gooseberry bushes. The rest of it was
whirling round and round the lawn with
all four Grannies chasing it. Satisfied,
Erg shut the window. He was determined
to finish his invention.

It was much trickier than he had
thought. The hole in the lid of the salt-
cellar was not big enough to get a straw
through. Erg had to enlarge it with the
skewer. And when he had got the straw
to go through, he could not get the

salt-cellar to stand properly upside down
on top of the machine. He had to bend
open the blades of the electric mixer to
hold it. And when he had done that, he
still could not get the blue water to go
plotterta-plotterta. It simply ran down
through the straw and into the inside
of the biscuit-tin. When Erg wound the
handle of the egg-beater, the water came
out of the holes in the tin in blue showers.

"Bother!" said Erg.

As he put more blue water into
the salt-cellar, he began to feel that
everything was getting out of hand.

The machine would not work. The earthy front of his pyjamas was blue and soaking, and so was most of the bathroom. And, to crown it all, there was a new outcry from the Grannies, from the kitchen this time. This was followed by feet on the stairs.

Next moment, all four Grannies were outside the bathroom door.

"Come out of there at once!" snapped Granny One.

"We're so worried, dear," hushed Granny Two.

"It was very unkind of you, dear,"

quavered Granny Four, "to fill the sugar bowl with salt."

But it was Granny Three who really alarmed Erg. "You know," she said, "that child has done something with Emily. I've not set eyes on her all the time I've been here."

Erg's eyes went guiltily to the sad face of the teddy in the bath.

Outside the door, Granny Two said, "I shall phone the Fire Brigade to get him out."

"And spank him when he is," Granny One agreed.

Erg listened to no more. He rammed
the salt-cellar and the straw back
in place and wound the egg-beater.
Pray pray pray praypraypray. Blue
water squirted. The works of the clock
sploshed. Round and round went the
chopstick, the mixer-blades, the salt-
cellar, the skewer, the
sardine-opener,
the mincer-
cutters, the
straw and the
clip off the
vacuum cleaner.

"Only one Granny," prayed Erg, winding desperately. "I can't manage more than one – please!"

Chapter Seven

There was a sudden silence outside the bathroom door. It's worked! Erg thought.

"Erg," said a large quavery voice outside. "Erg, open this door."

"In a minute," Erg called.

The words were hardly out of his mouth when the bathroom door leapt, and crashed open against the wall. The one Granny Erg had asked for came in. Only one. But Erg stared at her in horror. She was six feet tall and huge all over. Her hair was the baby pink of Granny Three's. Her face was the stern face of Granny One, except that it wore the worried look of Granny Two. Her voice was the quavery voice of Granny Four, but it was four times as loud. Erg knew at a glance that what he had here was all four Grannies in one. They had

blended into Supergranny. He jumped up to run.

Supergranny swept towards Erg. With one hand she caught Erg's arm in a grip of steel. At the same time, she was keenly scanning the rest of the bathroom.

"What is this mess?" she quavered menacingly. "And where is Emily?"

Erg dared not tell the truth. He avoided the teddy's accusing stare. "Emily went to play in the park," he said.

"Very well," said Supergranny. "We shall go and get her. Come along, dear."

"I can't go like this!" Erg protested, looking down at his earthy, blue, wet pyjamas.

All the Grannies were a little deaf when it suited them. Supergranny was super-deaf. "Come along, dear," she said. She plucked the teddy out of the bath and planted it in Erg's arms. "Don't forget teddy-weddy the fairies brought you." And she pulled Erg towards the door.

All Erg could think of was to spare one hand from the teddy and snatch up his invention from the wash-basin as he was pulled away. Blue water from it trickled down his legs as Supergranny towed him downstairs, but Erg hung on to it grimly. As soon as he got a chance, he was going to wind the egg-beater again and get Supergranny sent to Mars – which was surely where she belonged.

But, in the hall, Supergranny's piercing eye fell on the prayer-machine. "You can't take that nasty thing, dear," she said. She dragged it away from Erg and dropped it on the floor. Miserably, Erg tried dropping the teddy too. But Supergranny picked it up again and once

more planted it in Erg's arms. "Come along, dear."

Erg found himself in the street outside the house, in wet blue pyjamas, with one hand clutching a huge teddy and the other in the iron grip of Supergranny. Behind him, the front door crashed shut. Erg could tell by the noise that it had locked itself. "Have you got a key?" he said hopelessly.

All the Grannies were a little vague at times, when it suited them. Supergranny was super-vague. "I don't know, dear. Come along."

Erg knew he was locked out of the house and the prayer-machine locked in. As a last hope, he tried lingering beside Granny Three's snake green car. "Can we drive to the park?"

But three of the Grannies did not know how to drive, and that cancelled out the one who did. "I don't know how to drive, dear," said Supergranny.

So Erg was forced to trot along the pavement beside Supergranny. They kept passing people Erg knew. Not one of these people spared a glance for Supergranny. It was as if they saw

pink-haired super-women every day.
But every single person stared at Erg,
and Erg's pyjamas, and the huge teddy
bear. Erg tried to keep an expression on
his face of a boy playing woad-stained
Ancient British convicts, who had just
slain a fierce teddy bear. But, either
that was too hard an idea for one face
to express, or Erg did not express it very
well. Almost everybody laughed.

Erg was glad when they reached the
park and found it nearly empty, except
for some girls on the swings.

Here, Supergranny seemed to forget

they had come to look for Emily. But
that did not help Erg. Supergranny led
him over to the slide and the swings.
"You play, dear. Slide down the slide,
while I rest my poor feet." She sat
heavily on the nearest park bench.

Erg tried to defy her. "What if I don't
slide down the slide?" he asked.

"Awful things happen to little boys
who disobey," Supergranny quavered
placidly.

Erg looked her in the steely eye and
believed it. He leant the teddy against
the steps of the slide and began bitterly

to climb up. He knew that when he got to the top, the girls on the swings would see him and laugh too.

But when he got to the top of the slide, everyone had left the swings except one big girl. She was such a big girl that she had to swing with her legs stuck straight out in front of her. Erg sat at the top of the slide and stared.

That big girl was Emily.

Unbelievingly, Erg craned to look over his shoulder. The big yellow teddy bear was still leaning against the steps of the slide. Had the invention perhaps

not been a prayer-machine after all? Erg
looked hopefully over at the park bench.
Supergranny still sat there. Her pink
head was nodding in a super-doze.

Erg flung himself on the slide and
shot down it. He shot off the bottom and
raced across to the swings.

"Emily!" he panted. "What happened?
Where did you go?"

Emily gave Erg an unfriendly
look. "To have lunch with my friend
Josephine," she said. "Dear brother," she
added, and stood up against the swing
ready to shoot forward on it and kick

Erg in the stomach.

"Oh, be nice, please!" Erg begged her. "*Why* did you go?"

"Because you were so horrid to me," said Emily. "And then when I opened the front door, Granny Three was outside heaving a teddy out of her car, and I couldn't face her. I hate Granny Three. So I hid behind the door while she went to give you the teddy, and then I ran round to Josephine's."

So the teddy had come from Granny Three. It was all a terrible mistake. It was a natural mistake, perhaps, because

Granny Three had never been known
to give anyone anything before, but
a mistake all the same. And to make
matters worse, Supergranny had noticed
Erg was not sliding. She sprang up and
came scouring across to the swings,
calling for Erg in a long quavering hoot,
like a magnified owl. It was such a noise,
that people were running from the other
end of the park to see what was the
matter.

Erg watched her coming, feeling like
a drowning man whose life is passing
before him in a flash. The prayer-

machine had been working all along,
he knew now. He had not asked it to
turn Emily into a teddy-bear, but he *had*
asked it to send her away, and it did. It
had not needed blue water. It had made
the washing keep the Grannies busy
without. It was the chopstick that did
things. And, like all such things, Erg saw
wretchedly, as Supergranny pounded
towards him, it gave you three wishes,
and he had used all three. He had no
way of getting rid of Supergranny at all.

Emily stared at the vast, running
Supergranny. "Whoever is that?"

"Supergranny," said Erg. "She's all of them, and she's after me. Please help me. I'll never be horrible to you again."

"Don't make promises you can't keep," said Emily, but she let go of the swing and stood up.

Supergranny pounded up. "*There* you are, Emily!" she hooted. "I've been *so* worried!"

"I was only in the park," Emily said. "I think we'll go home now." She was, Erg was interested to see, nearly as large as Supergranny.

"Yes, dear," Supergranny said, almost meekly. And when Emily picked up the teddy and gave it to her, Supergranny took it without complaining.

They set off home. "How are we going to get in?" Erg whispered to Emily. "She's locked us out."

"No problem. I took the key," Emily said.

Halfway home, Supergranny's feet began super-killing her. She came over super-faint and had to lean on Erg and Emily. Erg had to stand staggering under her huge weight on his own while Emily fetched out her key and opened the front door.

"Good Lord!" said Emily.

The hall was full of dirty clothes. Dry dirty clothes were now galloping and billowing downstairs. Wet dirty clothes were crawling soggily through from the kitchen. Emily shot a horrified look at Supergranny and went charging indoors to catch the nearest pair of dirty jeans. She tripped over the invention in the middle of the floor. She fell flat on her face. *Crunch. Crack*. The egg-beater rolled out from one side in two pieces. The chopstick rolled the other way, *snapped in half*.

"*Ow!*" said Emily.

The clothes flopped down and lay where they fell. Supergranny's mighty arm seemed to disentangle itself between Erg's hands. It was suddenly four arms.

Erg let go, and found himself surrounded by the four Grannies, all staring into the hall too.

"Get up, Emily!" snapped Granny One.

"Oh, Erg!" said Granny Two. "Out of doors in pyjamas! You *are* growing up peculiar!"

"I shall take your teddy away again," said Granny Three. "Look at this mess! You don't deserve nice toys!"

"Let's have a nice cup of tea," quavered Granny Four. A thought struck her. She turned pale. "We can do without sugar," she said faintly. "It's better for us."

Erg looked from one to the other. He was very relieved, and very grateful to Emily. But he knew he was not going to enjoy the next three days.

Auntie Bea's
Day Out

"I shall take the children for a lovely day at the seaside tomorrow," said Auntie Bea.

The children felt miserable. Auntie Bea was huge, with a loud voice. She had been staying with the Pearsons for a

week then, and they all felt crushed and cross.

"You needn't bother to drive us, Tom," said Auntie Bea. "I can easily go by bus." This was Auntie Bea's way of telling Mr Pearson he was to drive them to the seaside.

Mr Pearson looked very cheerful. "Isn't that lucky? I have to take the car for its inspection tomorrow."

When Auntie Bea decided to do something, she did it. She turned to Mrs Pearson. "Well, you can help me carry the things, Eileen."

Mrs Pearson hastily discovered that she was going to the dentist.

"Then Nancy will help," said Auntie Bea. "Nancy's so sensible."

"No, I'm not," said Nancy.

"So that's all right," said Auntie Bea. She never attended to anything the children said. "Nancy can look after Debbie, and Simon can carry the things."

The number of things Auntie Bea needed for a day at the seaside would have been about right if she was going to climb Mount Everest. Mr Pearson helped her pile them in the hall, in twenty-two

separate heaps. Auntie Bea was so afraid
of losing or forgetting some of them that
she wrote out twenty-two labels, each
with their names and address on it, and
tied them to the bundles. Meanwhile,
Mrs Pearson cut up four loaves to make
the number of sandwiches Auntie Bea
thought they would need.

"And little jellies in yogurt cups,"
Auntie Bea said, racing into the kitchen.
"*Such* a good idea!"

Mrs Pearson was so glad to be getting
rid of Auntie Bea for a day that she
made them two jellies each.

"I feel like a human sacrifice," Simon said. "How does she think I can carry all that and manage Honey as well?" Honey was due to have puppies any day now. Simon was too anxious about her to leave her behind.

Auntie Bea came downstairs shaking out a vast swimsuit. It was electric blue with shiny orange hearts all over it. Nancy blinked, and wondered what Auntie Bea would look like wearing it.

"That's pretty," said Debbie, who loved bright colours. "I shall make Teddy a swimsuit like that."

"I hope it rains," said Nancy.

Unfortunately, the next day was bright and sunny. But they missed the early bus, because of Teddy and Honey. Debbie had pinned a scarf around Teddy like a nappy, and she had written him a label too: *Deb's Ted wiv care in Emurjunsy fone Millwich 29722.*

As soon as Auntie Bea saw Teddy, she said, "No, dear. We only take things we need today." Debbie's face took on its most mulish look, and the argument only ended when Auntie Bea saw Honey

drooping joylessly on the end of her lead.

"You can't take him, dear. He might have his puppies at any moment!" Just as Auntie Bea never attended to children, she never attended to whether dogs were she's.

The argument only finished when Simon found he could not carry all his bundles, even without Honey.

"You'll have to leave the stove and the kettle," said Mrs Pearson, very anxious to see them off.

"In that case, we must take plenty of boiled water!" said Auntie Bea. "Think

of the germs!"

So Simon's bundles were repacked and they set off to catch the later bus. Nancy went first with a light load of: one tartan rug, one carrier-bag of sandwiches, a first-aid box, and a bundle of buckets and spades. Auntie Bea sailed behind hung about with: one folding chair, one striped umbrella, three pints of milk, a bag of sweaters, a bag of suntan cream, a packet of sandwiches, two dozen hard-boiled eggs, a complete change of outsize clothes, three books, and a radio. Debbie trotted behind that with: a bundle of

 towels, a beach ball in
a string bag and
a basket full of
jellies and cake,
with Teddy
defiantly sitting
in it too. A long,
long way behind
came Simon. He was not sure what was
in the rucksack, nor what was in his other
six bundles, but he could see thermos
flasks sticking out of one and an electric
torch out of another. His knees buckled
under it all, and Honey kept tangling her

lead around them. Honey did not seem happy.

"It will serve him right if he has his puppies in the sea," Auntie Bea said, and counted the bundles to make sure they had remembered them all.

Nothing much happened on the bus ride, except that Honey threatened to be sick. When they got to Millhaven, it was quite late in the morning and already very crowded.

"Crowds, germs!" said Auntie Bea, counting everything again. "We should have caught the early bus." She hoisted

up her twelve bundles and set off happily down the steps to the sand, calling, "Don't bother to help with all this. I can manage perfectly."

They struggled after her down the steps and caught her up on the sand.

"Debbie," said Auntie Bea, "you take the umbrella. If Nancy takes the folding chair, I can manage perfectly."

"No, I won't," said Debbie. "It was you who brought it."

"Why don't we stop just here?" Nancy asked.

Debbie's refusal brought out the worst

in Auntie Bea. She gave a scornful look around at the deck chairs, rugs, and sand castles on the crowded beach, and called out to the man who hired the deck chairs in her loudest, most hooting voice: "My good man, can you direct me to somewhere less crowded?"

The deck chair man scratched his head. "Well, it thins out a bit up there, ma'am, but you can't go in the rocks. Tourists are not allowed on the island."

Auntie Bea stuck up her head indignantly at being called a tourist and set off at a trot where the man pointed,

hooting to the children to come along.
They ploughed after her, making zigzags
around the other families, who all stared,
because Auntie Bea kept turning around
and hooting at them. To the right were
the lovely white waves of the sea, rolling,
folding, and breaking with a joyful smash,
but Auntie Bea would not hear of stopping.
Honey, on the other hand, would not walk.
She had never seen the sea before. All she
knew was that it was the biggest bath in
the universe, and she dreaded baths. Simon
had a terrible time with her.

Nancy suggested that they stop for the

donkeys, and for the swings, and for one
of the ice-cream carts. But Auntie Bea just
cried out "Germs!" and scudded on. She
would not stop until they had left all the
people behind, and there was nothing but
rocks. There was a kind of road of rocks
stretching into the sea and, at the end of
the road, an island. It was quite small –
only big enough to hold a tuft of trees.

"The very place!" cried Auntie Bea,
and went out over the rocks like Steve
Ovett winning a race.

Honey, for some reason, was even
more afraid of the island than the sea.

Simon had to walk backwards, dragging her. When he turned around at the end, he found there was a barbed-wire fence round the island and a large notice on the gate: ISLAND ISLAND KEEP OUT.

There was no time to wonder about that. Auntie Bea was already charging through the trees. Simon dragged Honey past another notice: NO TRESPASSERS, and yet another: TRESPASSERS WILL BE SORRY. By that time, Auntie Bea had stopped and he caught up.

"I don't think we ought to be on this island," Nancy was saying.

"Nobody's afraid of three ignorant notices, dear," said Auntie Bea. "We're going to camp here."

Everyone was too tired to protest. They threw down the bundles and thankfully tipped the sand out of their shoes. Honey lay down, panting. She looked rather ill. Auntie Bea prepared to put on her swimsuit. First she spread the rug out. Then she arranged the chair and the screen and the umbrella to make a sort of hut. Finally, she crawled mountainously in to undress.

Nancy and Debbie undressed where

they were, and Simon tried to do the same. His shirt was stuck to his back by something sticky and smelling loudly of strawberry.

"I think the jellies have leaked on you," Debbie said, and crawled over to look at the yogurt cups in her basket. The sun had melted every one, and, in the mysterious way things happen at the seaside, every one was half full of sand. Teddy was soaked in strawberry juice. "This is *awful*!" said Debbie, and put Teddy on the branch of a tree to dry.

"Don't grumble, dear," Auntie Bea

called out of her hut. "We're having a *lovely* time!"

The island gave a curious shudder. It made them very uneasy.

"Auntie Bea," said Nancy, "I really think we ought to move."

"Nonsense, dear," called Auntie Bea.

At that, the island gave a bigger shudder and a heave. It felt as if they were going over a humpbacked bridge in a car. And everything was different.

There was a strong wind. They were all kneeling or standing on very short grass, shivering. There were no trees.

Teddy was hanging in the air above Auntie Bea's hut. They could hear the sound of waves crashing all around in the distance, from which they could tell they were on another, bigger island. But they had no idea where.

Almost at once, a hot man in a beret came panting up the green slope towards them. He was wearing a brown sweater with green patches on the elbows and shoulders. "I say!" he shouted. "You lot can't picnic here! You're right in the middle of a gun range there!"

The umbrella heaved. Auntie Bea

appeared, looking larger than ever. She

had her skirt around her neck like a

poncho. "Don't talk nonsense, my good

man," she said. The soldier stared at her,

and at Teddy hanging over her head. He

gave a sort of swallow. "We leave here

over my dead body," said Auntie Bea,
and dived back inside her hut.

"That's just what it will be—" the
soldier started to say, when the island
once more tried to shake them off – if
that's what it was doing. There was a
jerk, and they were on a small rock in the
middle of a lake.

"People don't order me about," Auntie
Bea remarked from inside her hut.

There was another jerk, and they were
somewhere dark, with water heaving
nearby. Honey began to shiver.

"We're having a lovely day!" Auntie

Bea asserted, from behind the umbrella.

The island jerked again, quite angrily, and it was freezing cold, but light enough to see by. There was frost or ice under their bare knees. The frosty space was rather small, and heaving, as if it was floating. The sea was very near, dark green, in frighteningly big waves.

"This is an iceberg," said Nancy, with her teeth chattering. "That's cheating."

"How many more kinds of island are there?" shivered Simon. "No, don't tell me. You'll put ideas in its head. Good dog, Honey."

"Oh!" Debbie shrieked. "Teddy's gone! I want to go home. Teddy!"

Auntie Bea, shielded from the ice by her blanket and screened from the view by her hut, called out, "Don't spoil our lovely day by screaming, dear."

The iceberg jerked, a bob of annoyance. They were on ice still, but this time it was the top of a mountain. Instead of water, they were surrounded by clouds.

"Teddy!" cried Debbie.

"Lovely day," repeated Auntie Bea.

Another jerk instantly flung them

into sweltering heat, somewhere low down and steamy. Water bubbled between their toes and brown water slid past a few feet away. Honey growled and Nancy gasped. An unmistakable alligator slid by with the water.

"I agree with Debbie," said Nancy. "I want to go home."

"Can't we shut Auntie Bea up?" Simon whispered. "She keeps annoying it."

"You'll feel better when you're in the water, dears," Auntie Bea called out.

Nancy was still shouting. "No!" when

they were pitched somewhere cooler, crowded among bushes under a tall tree. There seemed to be a river in front of them, and park railings beyond that. A banana skin fell heavily on Simon's head. He looked up to find that the tree was full of interested monkeys. Several of them came down to inspect Auntie Bea's hut.

To Simon's amazement, a small boy was staring at them through the railings. "Hey, Mum," said the small boy, "can I have a picnic on there too?"

"I want to go home too," Simon said

uncomfortably.

Two of the monkeys had decided that Auntie Bea's umbrella was fun. They tried to take it up the tree with them. Auntie Bea's hand appeared around the edge of it, slapping.

"Don't be so impatient, dears. I'm nearly ready."

The monkeys had barely time to chitter angrily before that island tossed them aside too. Auntie Bea's hut was suddenly in the middle of a neat flower bed. Debbie was rolling in red geraniums. There was a great deal of

noise all around, but it was not water. It sounded like traffic. Simon jumped to his feet. He was on a mound surrounded by cars and lorries. Faces were pressed against the windows of a passing bus, staring at him.

"We're on a traffic island now," he said. "In the middle of a roundabout."

Nancy stood up too. "What will it think of next? I say, Honey's not here!"

"Ready, dears," called Auntie Bea. She stood up out of her hut in her bathing suit. Simon was gazing around for Honey, but even he was distracted

by the sight. Auntie Bea was gigantic.
The flowers looked pale beside her.
She was like an enormous beach ball,
only brighter than a beach ball has any
right to be. The people going by in cars
could not take their eyes off her. The
bus ran into the kerb. Two cars drove up
on to the flower beds. Brakes squealed
and metal clanged all around the
roundabout.

Only Debbie was not distracted by
the sight. She was fond of bright colours.
"This is the roundabout at the end of our
road!" she said.

"Quick!" said Nancy.

"Run!" said Simon. "Before she says anything."

They raced down among the flowers. Behind them, Auntie Bea hooted, "I do think cars should be banned on beaches," and vanished from sight – which caused a further pile-up of cars.

Nancy, Simon and Debbie dodged between the cars and ran on, up their road and into their own house.

"Why are you back so soon?" asked Mrs Pearson. She did not seem to have gone to the dentist. "Where's Auntie Bea?"

She could not understand what had happened. All Debbie could think of was Teddy, last seen floating in the air over a soldier. All Simon could think of was Honey, last seen growling at an alligator. All Nancy could think of was that she was never going near another island – of any kind – as long as she lived. Neither Mr nor Mrs Pearson grasped that something truly odd had happened until the phone began to ring.

The first caller was very polite and very high up in the Army. They had Teddy, he said, on an island somewhere

in Scotland. Could
any of the Pearsons
please reveal the
secret formula that
made Teddy float
in the air? Was it
anything to do with
the strawberry juice
Teddy was soaked in?
When nobody could
tell him what made
Teddy float, the high-
up man said that it
certainly had military

importance, and would Debbie mind
if they kept Teddy for analysis? They
would send a new teddy.

"I want *my* Ted!" Debbie shouted, but
the Army said it was impossible.

The next person to phone was a
Swiss Mountain Guide, who had found
the beach ball on top of a mountain,

complete with the
label giving their
address. He
asked if they
wanted it back.
They never did

answer that, because a policeman called
just then, looking rather grim and asking
to speak to Auntie Bea. She had caused
a Breach of the Peace, he said, and left
her radio in the middle of Silas Street
roundabout. But nobody, of course, knew
where Auntie Bea was by then.

Almost straightaway, there was
a puzzled phone call from Iceland.
A trawler captain had found a bag
of Pearson sweaters floating on an
iceberg and wondered if there were any
survivors from the wreck. Mr Pearson
had just sorted that one out when

someone telephoned all the way from South America. His English was not very good, but he seemed to be saying that the water had ruined the battery in the electric torch. But he wanted to

assure them that the buckets and spades were quite safe and very useful.

"Ask about Honey," said Simon. But the person in South America had not seen a dog, nor even a satisfied-looking alligator.

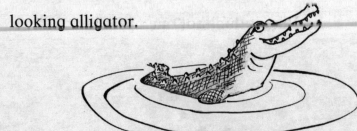

"Where's Auntie Bea, though?" Mrs Pearson kept asking. It was soon clear that Auntie Bea was still travelling. The Foreign Office phoned next. There was, they said, a mysterious complaint from the Russian Embassy. A basket full of jelly and sand in yogurt cups, with the Pearsons' address on it, had somehow appeared on the conning tower of a Russian submarine. The Russians were holding it for analysis. The Foreign Office wanted to know if they would find anything important in the yogurt cups.

"I don't think so," said Mrs Pearson

weakly. "They – they didn't find my sister as well, did they?"

But Auntie Bea had not been heard of. Nor had she been seen by an excited lady in Greece, who phoned next. This lady wanted the Pearsons to know that she was not so poor that she could not find two dozen hard-boiled eggs for herself, thank you. And she was throwing away the bag of clothes. They were too big for anyone on the island. She rang off before anyone could try to explain.

The American Embassy rang next.

Auntie Bea's umbrella had been found in the sea off Honolulu. They wondered if Auntie Bea had been drowned. So did the Pearsons. But since the next two calls were from Sweden and Japan, it began to look as if Auntie Bea was still being jerked from island to island.

Quite late that night, the London Zoo phoned. "It's taken us all this time to trace you," they said, rather injured. "The address fell off on our monkey island. How did you come to leave your dog there, anyway? The monkeys were trying to play with the puppies."

Mr Pearson said – a little wildly – that
he could explain everything. Then he
found that the zoo wanted him to collect
Honey and her six new puppies at once.
They were in the Children's Zoo. Simon

was greatly relieved. He went with his
father to fetch Honey, and did not mind
in the least when Honey was carsick,
though Mr Pearson did.

Meanwhile the others were still
answering the telephone, and there
was still no news of Auntie Bea. They
forgot what a trial Auntie Bea had been
and became worried. They had tender,
troubled thoughts about where she could
be. Nancy feared she was marooned on
a desert island like Robinson Crusoe, all
alone in her bathing suit. Debbie said
she was somewhere where they spoke

quite another language. Mrs Pearson
wrung her hands and said she *knew* Bea
was in China, under arrest.

Three days later, Auntie Bea rang
up herself. "You'll never guess, Tom!"
she hooted. "I'm in the Bahamas. I've
no idea how I got here, and I've had
to borrow money for the phone. You
needn't bother to come and get me,
Tom. I can manage."

Mr Pearson thought of all the phone
calls, and Debbie still in tears about
Teddy and – very crossly – about Honey
sick in his clean car. "I'm glad you can

manage, Bea," he said. "Come and see us when you get home." And he rang off.

If you liked FREAKY FAMILIES, you'll love: